Poppy
the Police
Horse

For Marilyn & Lyndon – G. P.
For Dylan, my super godson! – T. F.

First published in the UK in 2018
First published in the USA in 2018
by Faber and Faber Limited
Bloomsbury House
74–77 Great Russell Street
London WC1B 3DA

Designed by Faber and Faber
Printed in Malta

A CIP record for this book is available from the British Library

ISBN 978–0571–33778–1

2 4 6 8 10 9 7 5 3 1

Poppy the Police Horse

Gavin Puckett

Illustrated by Tor Freeman

ff

FABER & FABER

Hello, young reader . . . !

Thanks for taking the time,
In selecting my book of ridiculous rhyme.
I'm Gavin (you'll find my full name on
the cover),
The teller of tales, which you're soon to
discover.
It's taken me years to unearth these
strange fables,
By visiting farmyards and hanging round
stables,

And this is a series with just a selection,
Of some of the weirdest in my collection.
They're all about horses –
each one of them true –
And it's such a nice privilege to share
them with you!
Well, when I say *'True,'* I mean . . .
that's what I've heard.
(It's hard to believe, since they're all so
absurd!)
So, instead of returning this book to the
shelf,
Why not read on and decide for yourself?

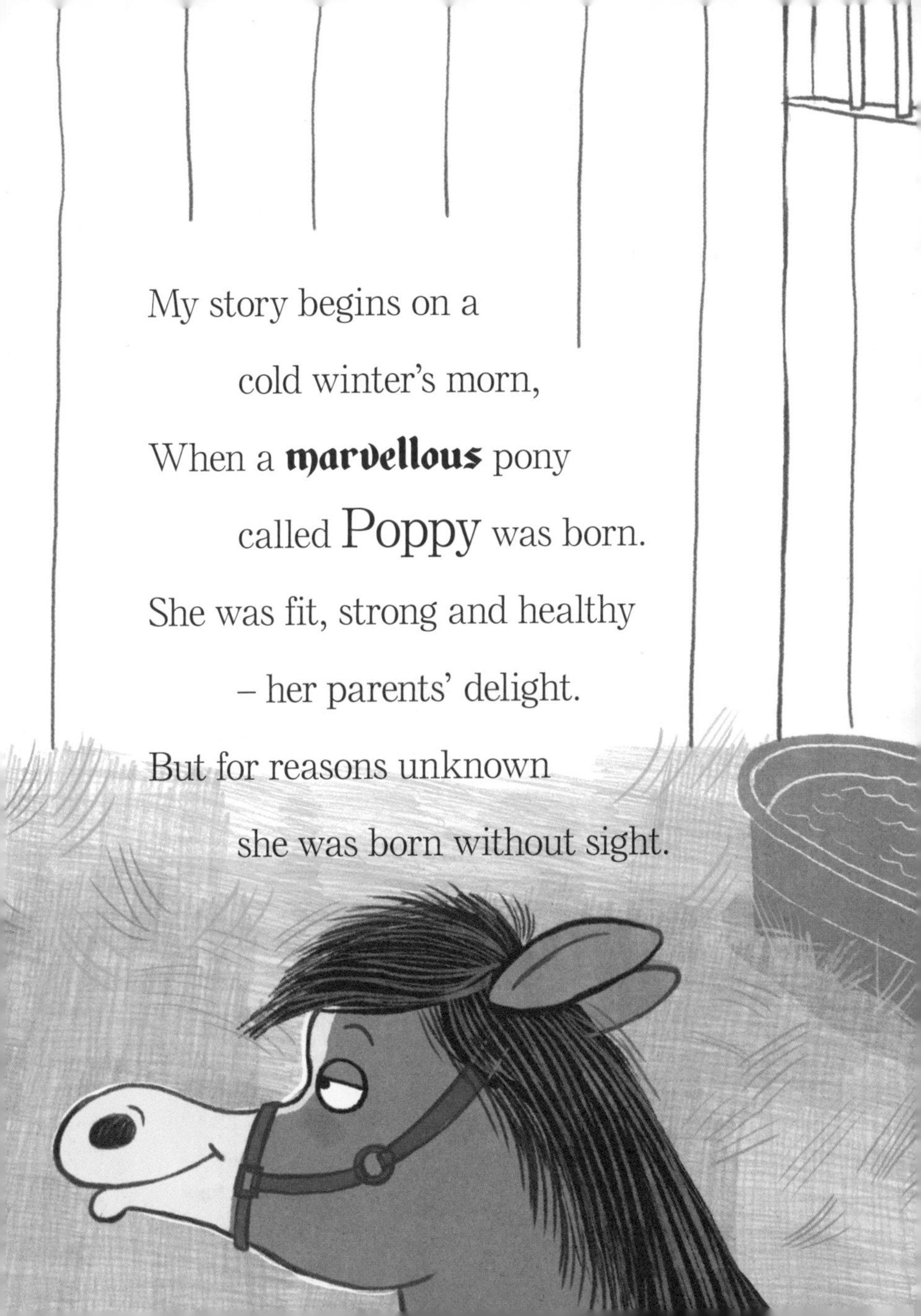

My story begins on a

cold winter's morn,

When a **marvellous** pony

called Poppy was born.

She was fit, strong and healthy

– her parents' delight.

But for reasons unknown

she was born without sight.

What she *did* have was

four very sensitive hooves,

And ears that detected

the *slightest* of moves.

She was able to gauge her

surroundings in haste –

Assisted of course

by a sharp sense of taste.

But Poppy's *real* talent

(her **GIFT**, I suppose)

Was the magical sense

that grew strong in her nose.

It was far more advanced than your

average foal;

Like the delicate snout of a

mouse or a mole.

In fact, people claimed

that this young horse's hooter,

Worked much like the brains of

a **SUPER-COMPUTER**.

Poppy picked smells up
wherever she went, and
Could work out an object
by *sniffing* its scent.
She could smell things a *mile* off,
like aeroplanes flying.

She could sniff
out the truth
when a person
was lying!

Poppy used **insight** to help her get by,

And saw everything clearly

inside her mind's eye.

If you met her, you'd never *believe*

she was blind.

This horse was remarkable – one of a kind!

One afternoon, **Chief Officer Rees**

(The person in charge of the local police)

Visited Poppy and said to the horse,

'A talent like
yours would be good
for the force!'

'We've heard of your nose,

your skills are ***sublime***.

Perhaps you could help us

in sniffing out crime?'

The officer smiled, and – fast as a rocket

– He whipped out a page he had stashed

in his pocket.

He began to tell Poppy some **key** information:

About a new paddock built next to the station.

Then he patted her nose and said, 'Here's
what I'll do . . .
Say yes, and we'll give this new stable
to you.'
Poppy's jaw dropped with this fabulous
news –
It was clearly an offer she couldn't refuse.
So, her hoof shook his hand, they both
smiled with delight,
And as easy as that – Poppy joined
up that night.

But it didn't take long for

her colleagues to find,

That 'work' was the last thing

on this horse's mind.

When Poppy moved in to that lovely

new build,

All of her dreams were completely fulfilled.

Her stable was **wonderful**, **stylish** and *gracious*

And each of the rooms was incredibly SPACIOUS.

Poppy adored it (without any doubt),

But her love for the place meant . . .

She never went out!

Poppy lounged in her stable all day

like a slob,

Not caring a **jot** for her

wonderful job.

Instead she drove each of the coppers

stir-crazy.

There were only two words to describe her:

PURE LAZY!

One morning, while Poppy
was dozing in bed,
PC Smith entered her stable and said,
'Poppy come help me, I'm terribly busy.
The phone hasn't stopped and my head's
getting dizzy...
'There are folks in this town who require
our assistance.
Please use your nose!' begged the man
with persistence.

RING RING!

But Poppy just stretched with a loud,
lazy groan.
‘Nah . . .’ sighed the horse. ‘Sort them out
on your own.’

Old Smithy huffed with a

shake of the head.

'I'll buy you a pie from next door!'

the man said.

(Next to the station lived Stanley the Baker,

Known in the town as the **finest**

pie-maker.

Smith knew too well what could lift

Poppy's mood:

The sweet taste of Stanley's

remarkable food).

STANLEY'S PIES
POLIC
BUS STOP
A
OPEN

'You're on!'

Poppy jumped up with no time to waste,

As her hungry tum *growled* at the thought

of a taste.

The policeman shot off in the blink of

an eye,

And soon he returned with a hot veggie pie.

It was the same one Poppy had seen in

her dreams –

Golden, with sauce oozing out from

the seams.

Old Smithy carried it off like a waiter.

'I'll put it down here –

you can eat

the pie later!'

First on their long list of

people to meet,

Was Mr Macdonald of

Harchester Street.

Macdonald had woken

that morning with shock:

It seemed that a burglar had

stolen his clock.

The man was incensed by

this terrible crime –

He had owned that antique for

a very long time.

This clock was an object that filled him
with joy,
As his father had bought it when
he was a boy.
Old Smithy asked questions and searched
round for clues,
Then he spotted some **tracks**, left by
somebody's shoes.

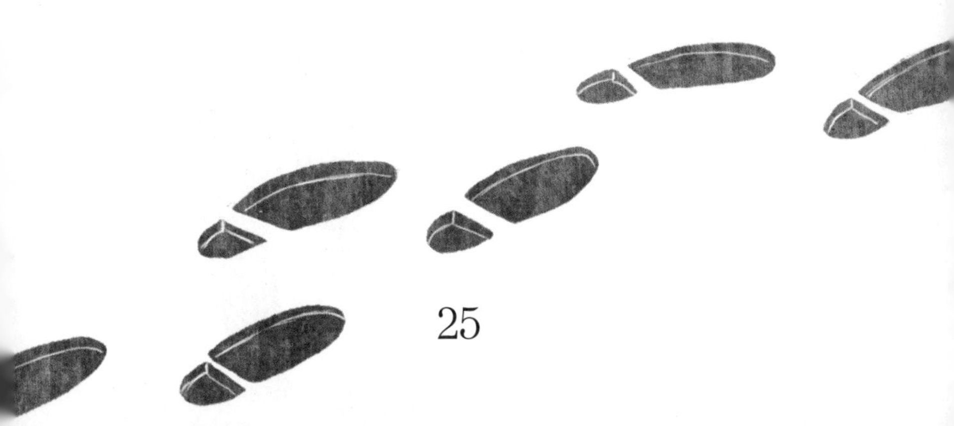

He called out to Poppy, 'Go sniff by

the shed.' Poppy just yawned.

'Nah . . . can't be bothered,'

she said.

Macdonald was dumbstruck. *This horse*
didn't care.
He spluttered and muttered and gasped
with despair.
The policeman was shocked and his face
turned **bright red**.
'We'll call back . . . excuse us . . .'
the officer said.
He clutched Poppy's reins and they
ambled away,
As Mr Macdonald looked on in **DISMAY**.

Poppy strolled on (at a *leisurely* pace),

Eventually stopping at Mrs Jones' place.

Mrs Jones had a fright – a

surprise without

warning –

When she tried to make

toast for her breakfast

that morning.

She picked up the kettle and gave it a fill,

And removed her two slices of toast

from the grill.

But on seeking a knife

to spread marmalade on –

She found her drawer EMPTY . . .

Her cutlery gone!

These utensils were not simply *any* old sort;
They were something the woman's late
mother had bought.
Each one was silver and **sparkly** clean –
And whenever she used them, she felt like
the QUEEN.

'I'm puzzled,' she sobbed. 'They were in
there before.'

As Smithy examined the windows and door,
He called to his horse (who was waiting
outside),

'Come, Poppy . . . let's catch this **villain**!'
he cried.

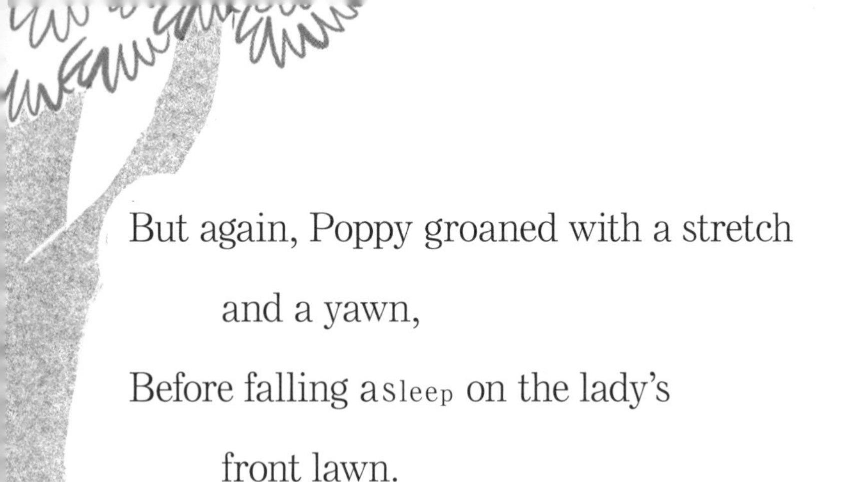

But again, Poppy groaned with a stretch

and a yawn,

Before falling asleep on the lady's

front lawn.

Mrs Jones spoke with a tear-filled yelp.

'I thought that you people were going

to **help**!'

PC Smith gulped before scratching his head.

'So sorry . . . we'll pop back in later,'

he said.

He ran to his horse, filled

with utter **FRUSTRATION**,

And shouted, 'Wake up!'

in complete desperation.

He nudged her, then **shook** her and prodded

her back.

But Poppy just snored as she

dreamt of her snack.

When she finally woke, Smithy gathered
her reins
With a feeling of rage flowing deep
in his veins.
'You're embarrassing me!' said the man
to his horse.
'Don't you have any *respect*
for the force?'

Sleepily, Poppy just carried on walking,

Failing to notice her colleague was talking.

Off they both trudged with a lazy **clip-clop**

To their next case at Mrs McGrath's

corner shop.

This poor old lady was feeling quite ill . . .

A villain had swiped all the

CASH from her till!

'My money's been taken!' the old

woman wept.

'The thief struck last night in my

shop as I slept!'

The policeman urged Poppy:

'Please *sniff* out a trail . . .

POLICE

But Poppy just **slouched** in the doorway instead.

'Is it time for my dinner?' the lazy horse said.

'TIME FOR YOUR DINNER . . . !?'
Old Smithy cried out,
As he snatched Poppy's reins and escorted
her out.
'I'VE HAD IT!' he shouted. 'THAT
DOES IT . . . WE'RE **THROUGH**.
NEVER AGAIN WILL I PARTNER
WITH YOU!'

Poppy now plodded back home with

a smirk.

'How perfect,' she muttered . . .

'I won't have to work!'

Deep in the shadows a *villain*

skulked home.

Through the shady back alleys, he walked

all alone.

This crook had a devious, mischievous smile,

Like the kind that you'd find on a sly

crocodile.

He had been out all night – getting up

to no good –

Swiping and stealing whatever he could.

He grinned as he carried his heavy brown sack,
Which was **bursting** with booty high up on his back.

But it seemed that his antics the
previous night
Had started to work up a
strong appetite.
His tum *rumbled* loudly and halted
his feet.
He'd been too busy thieving to take
time to eat.
Then . . . from a nearby window, of a
place he knew well,
His nostrils detected a **wonderful** smell.

He peered through the glass with a keen,

beady eye,

And licked both his lips as he spied

Poppy's pie.

Poppy walked home with her nostrils
flared wide,
She sniffed all the smells and felt happy
inside.

The aroma of donuts
breezed past her
cheek;

The whiff of fresh hot dogs
made both her
knees
weak.

She could even smell

vinegar drizzled

on fries,

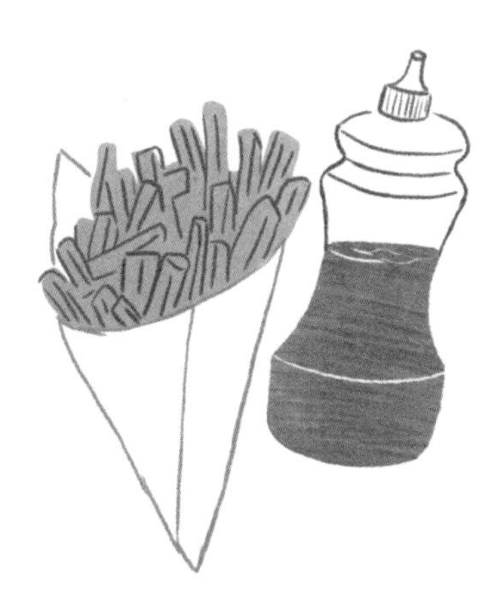

And a cake (in an

oven) just starting

to rise.

These scents jogged her memory of

what lay ahead

(A **pie** and a rest in her warm stable bed!).

When she got to the station, she felt
her pulse soar;
She galloped with *haste* through the
stable back door.

But Poppy discovered the facts early on.

Something *dreadful* had happened –

HER PIE WAS NOW GONE!

Poppy sniffed and she snuffled, she
searched low and high,
But someone had clearly *pilfered* her pie!
Old Smithy walked over and noticed
her frown.
'What's the problem . . . ?' he asked. 'You
look awfully down.'
Poppy looked up, her eyes heavy like lead.
'It's my **pie** . . .' the horse sobbed.
'It's been stolen!' she said.

PC Smith huffed as he ambled outside.

'Well, *I* can't be bothered to help!' he replied.

As his words echoed loudly

inside Poppy's head,

She remembered the self-centred

things she had said.

She recalled those poor people

affected by crime,

And how *she* had **failed** by

not giving them time.

Then something just clicked –

she'd not felt it before –

Her bottom shot upright,

her nose hit the floor.

POLICE
SNIFFER HORSE

In seconds, she'd picked up the scent
of her pie,
And was led to a small open window nearby.
The horse ran outside to the thin
window ledge,
And she followed that scent-trail
alongside a hedge.

She rummaged the ground like a

sniffer dog would.

(Though I doubt that a dog's nose

could be quite this good!)

She was focused, **alert** and at last in

the mood,

To sniff other aromas, besides

tasty food.

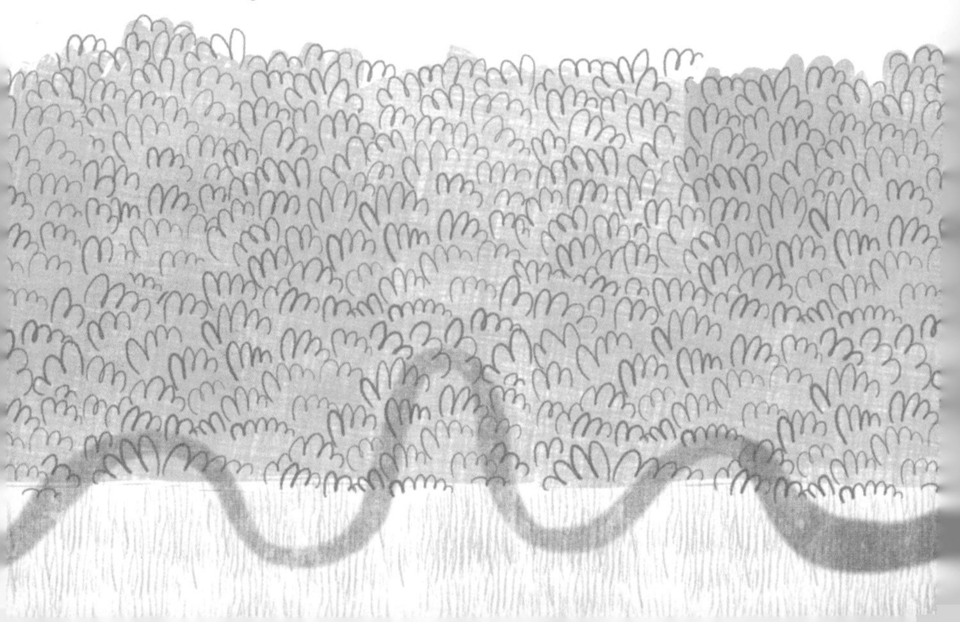

Her nose sensed the cash

from the old woman's store,

And the clock from the house

they had been to before.

She picked out the whiff of

the **silver** as well . . .

Along with a rather strange

villainous **smell**.

Old Smithy followed, in awe at the sound
Of the horse's keen nose as it scoured
the ground.

The scents soon grew stronger than ever before,

And they guided the horse to an old

crooked door.

The policeman crept silently (just like a mouse)

To a small windowpane at the rear of

the house.

He **wiped** off the dust, then peeped over

to look,

And inside he spotted **that**

mischievous crook.

(You've probably guessed – or at least
have a hunch –
What this devious rascal had planned
for his lunch.)
Licking his lips, full of pride and deceit,
The **villain** sat down at his table to eat.
Then . . . adjusting his mask with a glint
in his eye,
The crook jabbed a fork through the crust
of the pie.

From nowhere, a noise **boomed** behind the front door.

Then came a crash and an almighty **ROAARR!!!**

The thief jumped in terror (right out of

his skin),

As the front door burst open and Poppy ran in.

The horse showed her teeth as she stood

proud and tall,

Pinning that scoundrel against the cold wall.

'Please don't hurt me!' he begged,

consumed with sheer dread.

Poppy just smiled.

'You've been

busted!' she said.

The crook started crying,

his complexion

turned pale;

As he knew in his heart

he'd be sent off to jail.

PC Smith grabbed him and led him outside,

Where he placed him in handcuffs and

chuckled with pride.

Poppy sniffed round the kitchen, then out

to the hall,

Where a mountain of loot was piled up
by the wall.
There were things like **COMPUTERS**
and fifty-inch **tellies**.
Even bicycles, consoles and
fishermens' **wellies**.

Poppy reached for her pie with a
sorrowful frown,
She too had now suffered, like those
in her town.
In waltzed the officer, **BEAMING** with pride.
'I'm proud of you, Poppy – good work!'
the man cried.
'You deserve that nice pie,' uttered Smith
with a grin . . .
Then he gasped, as the horse
tossed the **pie** in the bin!

Poppy smiled at Old Smithy, shaking her head.

'There's no **time** for that – let's get working!'

she said.

To this very day, Poppy's out there,

still working,

Sniffing out ***villains*** wherever they're lurking.

Old Smithy's retired, but both remain friends,

And they often hang out and have fun

on weekends.

I'm told that (despite all the crooks

Poppy's caught)

Her *real* sense of **pride** lies in what

she's been taught.

At last she saw worth in her

marvellous gift,

And was happy supporting her pals

on the shift.

The main thing the horse came to realise

that day,

Was to **NEVER** let selfishness get in

her way.

She found 'helping others' could make
her walk tall,
But the 'desire to help' was the
best gift of all!